Click, Clack, peep!

# Click, Clack, Peep!

**Doreen Cronin**

*Illustrated by* **Betsy Lewin**

Ready-to-Read

Simon Spotlight

New York London Toronto Sydney New Delhi

SIMON SPOTLIGHT
An imprint of Simon & Schuster Children's Publishing Division
1230 Avenue of the Americas, New York, New York 10020
This Simon Spotlight edition February 2019 • Text copyright © 2015 by Doreen Cronin • Illustrations copyright © 2015 by Betsy Lewin
All rights reserved, including the right of reproduction in whole or in part in any form. SIMON SPOTLIGHT, READY-TO-READ,
and colophon are registered trademarks of Simon & Schuster, Inc. For information about special discounts for bulk purchases,
please contact Simon & Schuster Special Sales at 1-866-506-1949 or business@simonandschuster.com.
This Simon & Schuster Speakers Bureau can bring authors to your live event. For more information
or to book an event contact the Simon & Schuster Speakers Bureau at 1-866-248-3049 or visit our website at www.simonspeakers.com.
Manufactured in the United States of America 0719 LAK
10 9 8 7 6 5 4 3 2
Cataloging-in-Publication Data is available from the Library of Congress.
ISBN 978-1-5344-1386-3 (hc)
ISBN 978-1-5344-1385-6 (pbk)
ISBN 978-1-5344-1387-0 (eBook)

For Betsy and Ted
—D. C.

For little Ellis,
the newest "peep" in the Lewin clan
—B. L.

Click, Clack, Peep!

Farmer Brown stuck his head
out the window.
The farm was too quiet.
Everyone was watching
the egg.

Not a moo.
Not a click.
Not an oink.
Not a clack.

Not a baa.
Not a cluck.
Not a thing.

Then . . . a crack.

Inside the barn
everyone gathered closer.

# Baby Duck!

Baby Duck laughed.
peep peep peep
And laughed again.

Baby Duck waddled.
peep peep peep
And waddled again.

Baby Duck played.
peep peep peep
And played again!

The animals yawned.

peep peep peep

And yawned again.

The chickens sang a lullaby.

But Baby Duck would not sleep.

peep

peep

peep

But Baby Duck would not sleep.

# peep peep peep

# The sheep knitted a blanket.

But Baby Duck would not sleep.

The chickens went outside
to get some sleep.
The cows went outside
to get some sleep.

The sheep went outside
to get some sleep.
The mice went outside
to get some sleep.

Duck took off his headphones.

peep

peep

peep

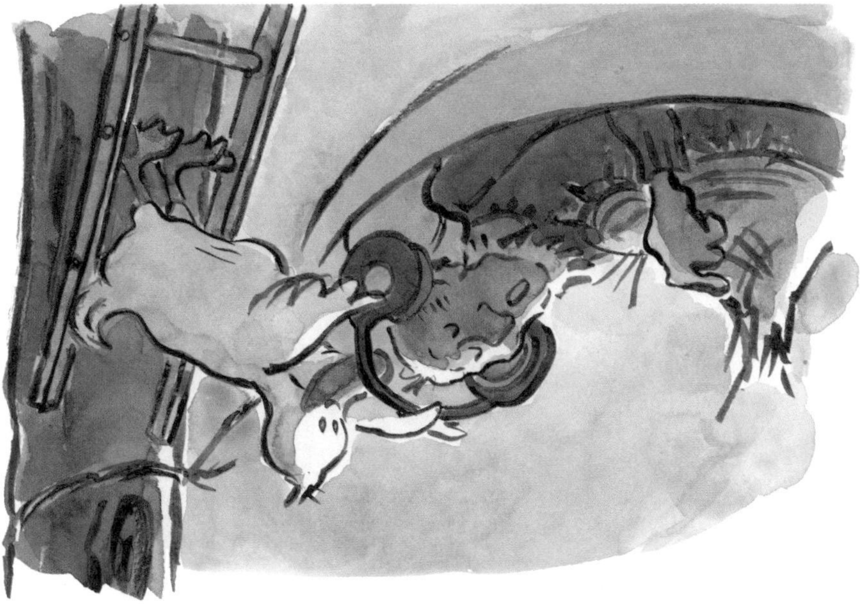

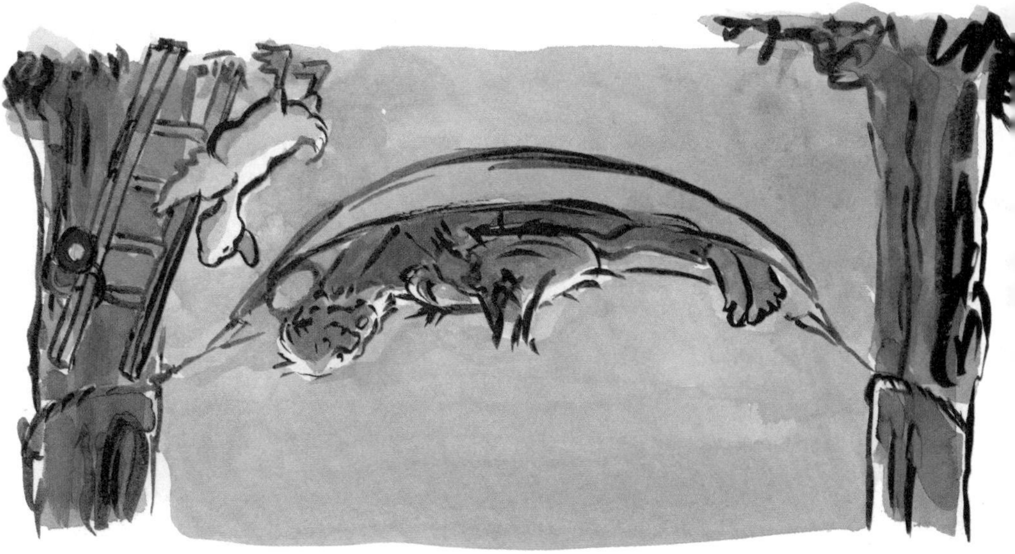

He put Baby Duck
into a bucket.

peep peep peep

He covered her
with a blanket.

peep peep peep

He carried her
outside.

peep peep peep

He climbed
into the tractor.

peep peep peep

He buckled up the seat belts.

peep peep peep

And backed out of the barnyard.
**beep beep beep**

He drove
back and forth.

peep
peep
peep

Back and forth.

peep peep peep

Back and forth.

peep, peep . . .

*...sleep.*

Farmer Brown opened his eyes
after a good night's sleep.

Not a moo.
Not a cluck.
Not a clack.

Not a peep.